First Printing

COPYRIGHT @ 2009 LANDMARK HOUSE, LTD.

Miles, David, 1987 -

International Standard Book Number: 978-0-9822874-3-9 (lib. bdg.)

Midwest Branch
Landmark House, Ltd..
1949 Foxridge Drive
Kansas City, KS 66106
913-722-0700

Southwest Branch
Kierland Corporate Center
7047 East Greenway Parkway
Scottsdale, AZ 85254
480-659-4052

Printed in China

PANEL OF JUDGES

Deborah J. Ellis
Katie Lohmann
Dr. Adolph Moser
Jayna Miller-Schneider
Jon Goodall Symon
Scot Symon
Teresa M. Melton-Symon
Nancy R. Thatch-Melton

EDITORS
Deborah J. Ellis
Nancy Thatch Melton

ASSISTANT EDITOR
Allyson Alvarez

ART DIRECTOR
Jayna Miller-Schneider

RESEARCH
Teresa M. Melton-Symon

PRODUCTION CO-ORDINATOR
Eric Taylor
Four Colour Imports

PUBLISHER
LANDMARK HOUSE, LTD.

BOOK FORMATTING
Patricia Prather
Rodger McReynolds

FINANCIAL SUPPORTERS
J.G. Symon & Companies

ADVISORS
Justin Benster
Arthur Malcy
Jack Mandelbaum
Norman Polsky
Robert Regnier

FOUNDER
David Melton

Creative Footprints for Kids

NOTE FROM THE PUBLISHER

Once in a great while, we receive a book into our contest that may need some more work, but it is almost print ready in its contest entry form. MRS. McFIG & HER VERY BIG WIG was indeed one of those books. When David Miles was rung up with the news that he had ranked first place in the 14 – 19 Age Category in the 2006 NATIONAL KIDS-IN-PRINT CONTEST, we had no idea at the time what a transformation this book would go through at the hands of its student author / illustrator. But change it did – from a terrific book to an even more spectacular book. David's creative brain tightened his rhyming text and took his paintings to an entirely different realm. The final version was a most magnificent piece of fun and witty writing matched perfectly with his colorful artwork.

David Miles is a most unusual young man. One of many children in his family, he grew up knowing how to multi-task -- keep several pans going in the fire and to get his work done. Aside from his studies at Brigham Young University and being a son, uncle and brother and talented artist and writer, 19-year-old David chose to take two years off from college to mission in Thailand. But before he left – during three short summer months, David completely redid MRS. McFIG and computer-programmed it into a ready-for-press format. Already adventurous in spirit and dedicated to his Mormon faith, David left the familiar to ride elephants in the Orient, learn a different language, eat exotic foods and help people in a distant land. Upon his return, David will waste no time in promoting his newly-published book and in resuming his collegiate studies. We have no doubt that -- whatever David Miles should want to do with his life from this point forwards – he is already starting out as a very accomplished young man. The world is the better for the time he gives it.

Not knowing how to any better lead up to or build up to the tremendous read you have in front of you, Landmark House, Ltd. has the distinct pleasure of introducing the first published book by David Miles:

MRS. McFIG & HER VERY BIG WIG!

TERESA M. MELTON-SYMON
President
Landmark House, Ltd.

Mrs. McFig
and the Very Big Wig

WRITTEN AND ILLUSTRATED BY

DAVID MILES

Creative Footprints for Kids

LANDMARK HOUSE, LTD.—Midwest
1949 Foxridge Drive
Kansas City, KS 66106
913-722-0700

LANDMARK HOUSE, LTD.—Southwest
7047 East Greenway Pkwy.
Scottsdale, AZ 85254
480-659-4052

In a small country village called Uppitydown . . .

Where cobblestone streets paved the bumpity ground,
There lived a rich widow named Mrs. McFig,
Who never left home without wearing a wig.

How rich was this lady? No person quite knew.
Some say there were orchards of jewels that she grew.
Her dresses were made of fine silk and fine lace.
She wore them with style and she wore them with grace.

But under her jewelry and very fine clothes,
McFig had a secret that nobody knows.
She feared that the people might giggle and stare,
If ever they knew that . . .

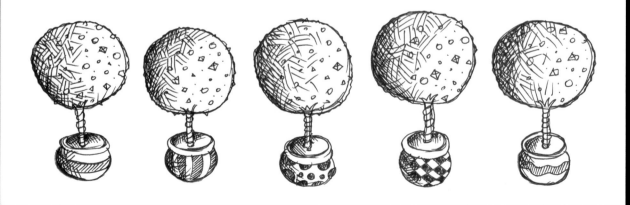

Her head was quite bare!

Not a hair on her head!
Not a haircut in years!

With a pink shiny noggin
right down to her ears,

It's really no wonder
that Mrs. McFig

Had Pompadour Pompous
come make her a wig.

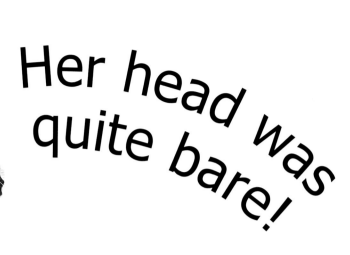

Up to the mansion he came in his cart,
A master, a genius, the best at his art.
"Good morning," he said as she opened the door,
"Just how can I help you? And what's the wig for?"

"I'm going to be married," McFig said with pride.
"And need a new wig that is fit for a bride.
My groom will be here from a faraway land.
He's sent me a letter to ask for my hand."

"I've never seen him and he's never seen me,
But surely he's noble and rich as can be.
So make me a wig that will dazzle this man!

It has to be stylish!
It has to be grand!"

And so while McFig nibbled cookies and cake,

And pictured the wig he was going to make,
Pompadour Pompous ran off to his cart,
And chose all the things that he'd need for a start.

He brought back some baskets of long golden hair
He cut it and curled it. He sewed it with care.
He wound silky ribbons around all the curls,
Then sprinkled bright stars and some silvery pearls.

"It's finished, it's perfect!" the wigmaker cried,
But Mrs. McFig said, "I'm not satisfied.
What if my groom is a famous French cook?
Add something to whip up a tastier look!"

So off to the kitchen and back at a sprint,
Came Pompadour Pompous with armfuls of mint,
Lemons and peaches and baskets of berries,
Apples and oranges and bushels of cherries.

But even with berries and stuffed like a pie,
McFig simply told him, "I'm not satisfied.
What if my groom is a brave, handsome knight?
My wig must be better — right now it's a fright!"

So out came a hatbox just filled to the top,

With finery bought at a fine ladies shop.
Powders and perfume and bottles of dye,
Things of all colors to spray and apply.

But after the glitzing and spritzing with dye,
McFig still insisted, "I'm not satisfied.
What if my groom is a merchant at sea?
This wig must be fixed — it's as bad as can be!"

So out to the garden the wigmaker went

To gather up roses for color and scent.

He snipped off six dozen,
then six dozen more,

Red ones and white ones
and pink ones galore.

Taller and taller, the wig grew quite high,
But still McFig shouted, "I'm NOT satisfied!

"What if my groom is a prince
with great powers?

Go find something else —
it's a mess full of flowers!"

So he opened a window and whistled a tune,

And down from the roof as the clock struck at noon,
Came fifteen fat birds, a feathery clan,
Of bluebirds and robins and one loud toucan.

But even with feathers and birds from the sky,
McFig simply hollered, "I'm NOT satisfied!
What if my groom is a wealthy, old king?
Find things that do more than just twitter and sing!"

So Pompadour Pompous ran down to the barn,

And lassoed a peacock
with leftover yarn.

He carted two piglets,
then three bleating goats,

And one stubborn mule
who was hungry for oats.

Bulging, near bursting,
the wig oinked and cried,

But still McFig bellowed,
"I'M NOT SATISFIED!"

"This wig still needs more!
Find something to fit!"

But Pompadour shouted,

"I give up!
I quit!"

He scampered away,
didn't pause, didn't stop,

But sped back to town
and his wigmaking shop.

He hurried inside and
he bolted the door,

And hoped not to see
that McFig anymore!

But back at the mansion,
McFig was still frantic.

"I'm late for my wedding!"
she cried in a panic.

"This wig isn't perfect,
that's certainly true.

"But time's running out.
It will just have to do!"

She dashed to the church
and attempted a smile

For there stood her groom
at the front of the aisle.

She straightened her wig, feeling just like a queen —

But then something happened, a very bad thing...

The mule tried to munch on the tiny goat's tail,
Who kicked at the peacock, who let out a wail,
Which startled a piglet, who jumped in surprise,
And snapped all the ribbons and broke all the ties.
McFig tried to stop them, but each time she tried,
The wig shook and shuddered, then swayed to one side...

Down came the peacock, the piglets, and goats.

Down came the mule that was looking for oats.
Down came the birds from their high, golden nest,
Down came the toucan and all of the rest.
Down came the lemons and peaches and cherries,
Down came the apples and oranges and berries.
Down came the roses, the stars, and the pearls,
Down came the ribbons and long, golden curls.
Down it all came in an unraveled heap
That covered the groom nearly seven feet deep!

McFig started sobbing, tears streamed down her face.
"My secret is out!" she declared in disgrace.
"I'll never get married, I'm bald like a pig,
And now my poor groom is beneath this new wig!"

But then from the rubble, McFig heard a shout,
And wonder of wonders, the groom's head popped out!
"Dear madam!" he called from the front of the room,
"We'll still have this wedding. I'll still be your groom!"
"I know I'm not all that you thought I would be,
Not famous or wealthy, not high royalty.
I'm not all that dashing. No fairytale look.
No king, prince or merchant, no knight and no cook."

"I'm none of these things, but I'm still right for you,

'Cause guess what, my dear…"

I'm completely bald too!

Creative Footprints for Kids

LANDMARK HOUSE, LTD.